Thomas
Story Treasury

The Rev. W. Awdry and Christopher Awdry

First published in this edition 1999 by Egmont Children's Books Limited
239 Kensington High Street, London W8 6SA

Thomas Comes to Breakfast
by the Rev. W. Awdry
First published in Great Britain in 1985
This adaptation first published 1998 by Egmont Children's Books Limited
239 Kensington High Street, London W8 6SA
New line illustrations by Robin Davies

Thomas and Gordon off the Rails
by the Rev. W. Awdry
First published in Great Britain 1990
This adaptation first published 1999 by Egmont Children's Books Limited
239 Kensington High Street, London W8 6SA
New line illustrations by Robin Davies

Thomas and the Hurricane
by Christopher Awdry
First published in Great Britain 1992
This adaptation first published 1999 by Egmont Children's Books Limited
239 Kensington High Street, London W8 6SA
New line illustrations by Robin Davies

THE BRITT ALLCROFT COMPANY

1 3 5 7 9 10 8 6 4 2

ISBN 0 434 80543 2

Printed and bound in Great Britain

Contents

Thomas Comes to Breakfast

The Rev. W. Awdry
Illustrated by Robin Davies

Thomas the Tank Engine has worked his branch line for many years. "You know just when to stop," laughed his Driver one day. "You could almost manage without me."

Thomas didn't understand that his Driver
was only joking. "Driver says that I don't
need him anymore," he told the others.

"Don't be so silly," said Percy.
"I'd never go without my Driver,"
said Toby earnestly. "I'd be frightened."

"Pooh!" boasted Thomas. "I'm not scared.
Just you wait and see."

It was dark in the morning when the Firelighter came to light the engines. Thomas drowsed comfortably as the warmth spread through his boiler.

He woke again in daylight. Percy and
Toby were still asleep.
"I'll give those silly stick-in-the-muds
a surprise," he chuckled.

He felt steam going into one piston, and then to the other. "I'm moving! I'm moving!" he whispered. "I'll creep outside and stop. Then I'll wheesh loudly to make them jump."

Thomas thought he was clever, but really he was only moving because a careless cleaner had meddled with his controls. He tried to wheesh, but he couldn't. He tried to stop, but he couldn't. He just kept rolling along.
"Never mind, the buffers will stop me," he thought hopefully.

But that siding had no buffers. The rails ended at the road. Thomas' wheels left the rails and crunched the tarmac. Ahead of him was a hedge, a garden gate and the Stationmaster's house.

The Stationmaster and his family were having breakfast.
It was their favourite one of bacon and eggs.
"Oh horrors!" exclaimed Thomas as he shut his eyes and
plunged through the hedge.

There was a crash, the house rocked, plaster peppered the plates. Thomas peered through the broken window. He couldn't speak.

The **Stationmaster** strode outside. He shut off the steam and surveyed his wrecked garden.

His wife picked up the plates. "You miserable engine," she scolded, "just look at our breakfast – covered in plaster. Now I shall have to cook some more." She banged the door behind her.

They finished their breakfast in the kitchen and left Thomas sulking on his own. More and more plaster fell. Thomas wanted to sneeze, but he didn't dare in case the house fell on top of him.

No one came near him for a very long time – everyone was much too busy. At last some workmen arrived to prop the house up with strong poles.

Next they brought a load of sleepers and made a road over the garden so that Donald and Douglas, puffing hard, could pull Thomas back to the rails again.

Thomas looked so comic that the twins laughed aloud.
"Goodbye Thomas," they chuckled. "Don't forget your
Driver next time!"
His Driver and Fireman began to tidy him up.
"You're a perfect disgrace," they told him.
"We're ashamed of you."

"And so am I," said a voice behind them.
"You're a very naughty engine," The Fat Controller
continued.
"Yes, Sir. I'm sorry, Sir," faltered Thomas.

"You must go to the Works to be mended, but they've no time for you now. Percy will take you to a siding where you can wait till they are ready."

Next day a diesel railcar came.
"That's Daisy," said The Fat Contoller. "She's come
to do your work. Diesels never run off to breakfast
in Stationmaster's houses."
And he walked sternly away.

Thomas didn't enjoy his time at the Works.
"It's nice to feel mended again," he said afterwards,
"but they took so many of my old parts away and
put new ones in, that I'm not sure whether I'm really
me or another engine."

When Thomas came home, he soon made friends with Daisy. In fact, Thomas is glad to have her help with his passengers. He is now never so silly as to think he can manage without his Driver.

Thomas and Gordon off the Rails

The Rev. W. Awdry
Illustrated by Robin Davies

"Wake up, Gordon," said his Driver one morning.
"You've got a special train to pull, today."
"Is it coaches or trucks?" asked Gordon.
"Trucks," said his Driver.

"Trucks!" grumbled Gordon. "I won't go. I won't go!"
Gordon began to sulk and his fire wouldn't burn
properly. When Edward pushed him to the turntable,
he didn't help at all.

Gordon hissed loudly. "Trucks! I'll show them." And when
the turntable was half-way round, he moved slowly forward.
He only meant to go far enough to jam the turntable,
but once he was moving forward he found he couldn't stop.

"Whoosh," he said as he went right off the rails,
slithered down a bank and landed in a ditch.
The Yard Manager was very cross.
"Look what you've done, you silly great engine!"
he bellowed. "It will be hours before we can get
you out of here."
"Glug," said Gordon, apologetically.

It was dark when the breakdown gang came for Gordon.
They brought floodlights and powerful jacks. A crane lifted
Gordon's tender clear and then the workmen attached
strong cables to the back of his cab.

Then the men built a ramp of sleepers and James and Henry, pulling hard, managed to get Gordon back on to the rails. "Not such a splendid engine now, are you?" teased a workman. It was true. Gordon was very wet, very dirty, and he smelt awful!

A few days later, Thomas was at the junction
when Gordon arrived with some trucks.
"Pooh!" remarked Thomas to Annie and Clarabel.
"Can you smell a smell? A funny, musty sort of smell?"

"No," said Annie and Clarabel. "We can't smell a smell."
"Do you know what I think it is?" said Thomas, staring
at Gordon. "It's ditch water!" But before Gordon
could answer, Thomas had quietly puffed away,
giggling to himself.

Later, Thomas took some empty trucks to a mine. Long ago, miners digging for lead had tunnelled into the ground. One of the tunnels went right under the railway line and the ground above was weak.

At a fork in the sidings, a large notice board said,
"DANGER. Engines Must Not Pass This Point."
Thomas had often tried to get past, but he had
never succeeded. Today, though, he had a plan.
As his Fireman got out to change the points,
Thomas' Driver leaned out of the cab to see
where he was going.

"Now!" said Thomas to himself and, bumping the trucks fiercely, he jerked the driver off the footplate. "Stupid old board, there's no danger," he said as he followed the trucks past the board. There was a loud rumbling sound and the ground in front of Thomas started to cave in.

"Look out!" shouted Thomas' Driver. The Fireman scrambled into the cab and put Thomas' brakes on. But it was too late. "Fire and smoke!" shouted Thomas, "I'm sinking." And he was. The rails broke and he slid into the pit below.

"Oh dear," Thomas said. "I am a silly engine."
"And a very naughty one, too," said a familiar voice behind him. "I saw you!"
"Please get me out, Sir," said Thomas. "I won't be naughty again."
"I'm not so sure," said The Fat Controller. "We can't lift you out with a crane. The ground isn't firm enough. We might have to leave you there for some time …"
"Leave me … here?" wailed Thomas.

The Fat Controller thought for a while. "Hmmn,"
he said, "I wonder if Gordon could pull you out."
Thomas stumbled out a reply, "G – G – Gordon?"
He wasn't sure he wanted to see Gordon again
just yet.

When Gordon heard about Thomas' accident, he laughed loudly.
"Down a mine is he?" he asked James and Edward. "How fitting – I always said that he was a minor engine. Ho-Ho-Ho!" But he hurried to the rescue all the same.

Gordon reached the mine and carefully drew up behind Thomas.
"Poop-poop, little Thomas, have you got that sinking feeling?" he whistled. "We'll have you out of there in a couple of puffs."

Workmen fastened strong cables between the two engines.
"Are you ready?" called The Fat Controller.
"One, two three, HEAVE."
Very slowly and very carefully, Gordon pulled Thomas
back on the rails to safety.

"Thank you for rescuing me," said Thomas to Gordon,
"I was in a bit of a hole!"
His Driver and Fireman checked him over to see
where he was hurt. "I'm sorry I was cheeky."

"That's all right, Thomas," said Gordon.
"You made me laugh. I like that."
Then he whispered carefully, "I'm in disgrace,
you know, and it cheered me up."

Gordon started to tow Thomas back towards Tidmouth.
"I'm in disgrace, too," said Thomas as they started
their journey.
"Why! So you are, Thomas," Gordon replied. "We're both
in disgrace. Shall we form an alliance?"
"An ally – what?" asked Thomas.
"An alliance, Thomas. United we stand, together we fall,"
said Gordon grandly. "You help me and I'll help you."

"Right you are," said Thomas.
"Good! That's settled, then," rumbled Gordon.
And buffer to buffer the allies puffed home.

Thomas
and the
Hurricane

Christopher Awdry
Illustrated by Robin Davies

A howling gale was blowing across the Island of Sodor. None of the engines got much sleep that night.

"Brrr!" shivered Thomas as he struggled to wake up in the morning. The wind was cold as well as strong – it blew leaves and litter into the Shed.

There weren't many passengers that morning.
They all wanted to stay indoors and Thomas
didn't blame them.
"Lucky things," he thought.

But when Thomas reached the station by the river, he was astonished to see footballers playing in the nearby field. One team was wearing red shirts, while the other was in blue.

"It's part of the Knockout Competition," explained the Fireman. "At the end of the season, the winners will get a silver cup."

The trees between the field and the railway waved
wildly in the wind.
"Sooner them than me," Thomas muttered to himself.
"They'll all get knocked out if they're not careful!"

James was waiting at the junction. He didn't mind the wind, he said, and was even boasting about it. "My train was right on time," he announced proudly. "A little bit of wind can't stop me."

Just then the wind blew so hard that the station roof
shook ... and so did something else.
"Just look at that signal!" exclaimed Thomas.

"Signal – what signal?" James asked. Suddenly,
the signal gantry wasn't there any more. The
gale had blown it down.

"Help!" said Thomas in alarm,
as two more signal posts broke
and crashed to the ground.
"Let's get away from here."

The Fireman hurried to the signal-box
to find out what they should do.
"We can't move without any signals,"
explained the Driver.
"How do we know if it's safe?"

"Well, it's not safe here either," snorted James. "That's no wind, it's a hurricane!"

The Drivers laughed, but they did move the engines along the platform as far as they dared.

It was lucky that they did, because two minutes later the wind lifted the platform canopy clean off its framework and dropped it, to shatter on the platform below.

No one was hurt as the canopy crashed down, but Annie and Clarabel were very badly frightened, and some splinters of wood scratched Clarabel's paint.

At last a man with flags came and signalled
the two trains away.
James forgot his boasting and was only too glad
to get away. Thomas followed closely behind.

Thomas had the wind behind him now, and by the
time he reached the curve near the football
ground he was steaming along well.
They were halfway round the bend when suddenly
there was a jerk, and the Guard's emergency
brake went on hard.

"Ooooooooer," groaned Thomas.
"What's the matter now?"
He soon found out. Lying
across the line in front of him
were several enormous fallen trees.
Thomas' brakes bit hard and he
stopped just in time.

The Driver looked back. Running towards them were three footballers followed by the Guard who was waving his flag and blowing his whistle.

"So that's how the Guard knew when to brake,"
thought Thomas. "Thank goodness you stopped,"
panted the footballers when they arrived.
"We thought we were too late."
"It was a near thing," said the Driver.
"Thank you for warning us."

Later that day, Terence the Tractor came and dragged the trees off the line. Trevor was busy in the field using his circular saw to cut up the wood, while Toby and Percy worked hard all day taking the logs away.

Evening came and the line was clear, at last. Thomas, and Annie and Clarabel could go home.

A week later there was a party at the riverside
station. The Fat Controller gave all the footballers
a silver cup as a thank-you for saving the train.
"You may not have won the tournament," he
laughed, "but you certainly beat that hurricane!"